When Moon Fell Down

by Linda Smith
illustrated by Kathryn Brown

HarperCollins *Publishers*

When Moon Fell Down
Text copyright © 2001 by Linda Smith
Illustrations copyright © 2001 by Kathryn Brown
Printed in the U.S.A. All rights reserved.
www.harperchildrens.com

Library of Congress Cataloging-in-Publication Data
Smith, Linda, date
When Moon fell down / by Linda Smith ;
illustrated by Kathryn Brown.
p.   cm.
Summary: The moon falls down to earth one
night and roams about with a friendly cow before
returning to the sky.
ISBN 0-06-028301-7
ISBN 0-06-029497-3 (lib. bdg.)
[1. Moon—Fiction.   2. Cows—Fiction.
3. Stories in rhyme.]   I. Brown, Kathryn, date, ill.
II. Title.
PZ8.3.S6542 Wh 2001   00-33580
[E]—dc21   CIP
                                                          AC

Typography by Stephanie Bart-Horvath
1 2 3 4 5 6 7 8 9 10
❖
First Edition

To my dad, George, who loved the night,
and my children, Angella, Kali, Danny,
Annie, Christopher, Benjamin, Charlie,
and Alexander

                                        —L.S.

For Joe
    —K.B.

Moon

Fell

Down

One

Night . . .

Fell upon a farmer's lawn,
Rolled about in sheer delight
On fields he'd only shined upon.

The rye smelled sweet,
The night winds whirled,
Circling Moon in a misty
   wreath,
And he beamed in awe
At this wondrous world—
The stars above and earth
   beneath.

He'd never seen the trunks of trees
Or blades below the farmer's plow.

Moon didn't know a horse had knees,
But things were strangely sideways now.

Beyond the fence there came a cow,
Who boldly nibbled at his side.

The old moon laughed and took a bow

And offered her a golden ride.

They blew beyond the farmer's light,
Rolled up hills and floated down.
The hound dogs howled at the curious sight,
As Moon and Cow trespassed their town.

The city shops Moon knew quite well
For he'd lit upon each shingled top.
But what they sold he couldn't tell,
So now he paused to window-shop . . .

As did Cow at the garden store.

She ambled up to rattle locks,

But when she couldn't budge the door,

She ate the rose in the window box.

Moon fell in love with a blinking sign,
Cow poked around the milkman's cart.

Both thought the cheese shop just divine—
Each half-moon slice a work of art.

They wandered to and floated fro,
Up the sidewalks, down,

And with the moonlight's golden glow
They painted that small town.

Moon returned with Cow at dawn,
Rolling in with sleepy eyes.

Found Farmer pacing on his lawn,
Much to Cow's surprise.

"Moon!" he cried. "This isn't right!
Cow, how dare you roam!
A moon belongs in the sky at night,
And a cow belongs at home."

Cow ran off to the barn to fret,

Moon rose above the town,

But neither one would ever forget

The night when

Moon

Fell

Down.